THIS WALKER BOOK BELONGS TO:

_____

_____

_____

_____

First published as *Floss* (1992) and *Emma's Lamb* (1991)
by Walker Books Ltd, 87 Vauxhall Walk
London SE11 5HJ

This edition published 1999

2 4 6 8 10 9 7 5 3 1

This book has been typeset in Monotype Bembo.

Printed in Singapore

British Library Cataloguing in Publication Data
A catalogue record for this book is
available from the British Library.

ISBN 0-7445-6703-3 (hb)
ISBN 0-7445-6379-8 (pb)

# Floss
## —— & ——
# Emma's Lamb

## KIM LEWIS

WALKER BOOKS
AND SUBSIDIARIES
LONDON • BOSTON • SYDNEY

For John Mitchell
and Floss

# Floss

loss was a young Border collie, who belonged to an old man in a town. She walked with the old man in the streets, and loved playing ball with children in the park.

"My son is a farmer,"
the old man told Floss.
"He has a sheepdog
who is too old to work.
He needs a young dog
to herd sheep on his farm.
He could train a
Border collie like you."

So Floss and the old man
travelled, away from
the town with
its streets and houses
and children playing ball
in the park.
They came to the
heather-covered hills
of a valley, where nothing
much grew except sheep.

Somewhere in her
memory, Floss knew
about sheep.
Old Nell soon showed
her how to round them up.
The farmer trained her
to run wide and lie down,
to walk on behind,
to shed, and to pen.
She worked very hard
to become a good sheepdog.

But sometimes Floss
woke up at night,
while Nell lay sound asleep.
She remembered
about playing with
children and rounding up
balls in the park.

The farmer took Floss
on the hill one day,
to see if she could gather
the sheep on her own.
She was rounding them
up when she heard a sound.
At the edge of the field
the farmer's children were
playing, with a brand new
black and white ball.

Floss remembered
all about children.
She ran to play with
their ball. She showed
off her best nose kicks,
her best passes. She
did her best springs
in the air.
"Hey, Dad, look at this!"
yelled the children.
"Look at Floss!"
The sheep started
drifting away.

The sheep escaped
through the gate and
into the yard. There
were sheep in the garden
and sheep on the road.
"FLOSS! LIE DOWN!"
The farmer's voice
was like thunder.
"You are meant for
work on this farm,
not play!"
He took Floss back to
the dog house.

Floss lay and worried
about balls and sheep.
She dreamt about
the streets of a town,
the hills of a valley,
children and farmers,
all mixed together,
while Nell had to round
up the straying sheep.

But Nell was too old
to work every day,
and Floss had to learn to
take her place.
She worked so hard
to gather sheep well,
she was much too tired
to dream any more.
The farmer was
pleased and ran Floss
in the dog trials.
"She's a good worker now,"
the old man said.

The children still wanted
to play with their ball.
"Hey, Dad," they asked,
"can Old Nell play now?"
But Nell didn't know
about children and play.
"No one can play ball
like Floss," they said.
"Go on, then," whispered
the farmer to Floss.
The children kicked the
ball high in the air.

Floss remembered
all about children.
She ran to play with
their ball.
She showed off her
best nose kicks,
her best passes.
She did her best
springs in the air.

*For Sara and my mother*

# Emma's Lamb

One rainy spring morning at lambing time,
Emma's father put a little lost lamb in a box
by the stove. Then he went back
to the field to look for Lamb's mother.

Lamb and Emma looked at each other.
"Baaa," said Lamb, sitting up in his box.
Emma wanted to keep little Lamb
and look after him all by herself.

So Emma dried Lamb
because he was very wet.
She tried to keep him warm
because he was very cold.
Emma fed Lamb
because he was very hungry.

When Lamb was dry and warm and fed,
he and Emma played.
"Baaa," said Lamb, getting
into a mess.

Then Emma took Lamb for a walk
and he skipped along behind her.
Emma decided to play hide and seek.
She closed her eyes and counted to ten.
"Here I come!" she cried.

Emma looked for Lamb in the stable.
She looked for him in the barn.
She looked for him in the granary.
She looked all around the yard.

She couldn't find Lamb in the house.
He wasn't in his box.
She couldn't find him in the
sheep pens either.
"I give up!" she shouted.

But Lamb was nowhere to be found.
Emma didn't want to play any more.
She wanted Lamb to come back.
She thought he might be cold and hungry.
"Where are you, Lamb?" she cried.

"Baaa," came a sound from the hayshed.
Emma ran inside to look.
Lamb sat up in the nesting box,
where the hens had laid their eggs.
"Baaa," he cried and ran to Emma.

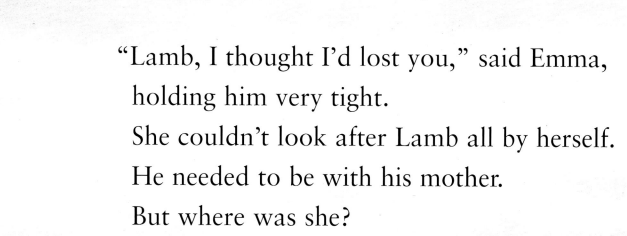

"Lamb, I thought I'd lost you," said Emma,
holding him very tight.
She couldn't look after Lamb all by herself.
He needed to be with his mother.
But where was she?

Then Emma saw her father across the field.

A ewe without a lamb ran ahead of him, calling.

"Baaa," cried Lamb. He wriggled to get free.

Emma put him down,

and Lamb ran as fast as he could to his mother.

Emma went to the field the very next day.

When she called, Lamb came running to see her.

"Will you remember me?" asked Emma.

Lamb and Emma looked at each other.

"Baaa," said Lamb, waggling his tail.

# MORE WALKER PAPERBACKS
## For You to Enjoy

Also by Kim Lewis

### THE SHEPHERD BOY
Shortlisted for the 1991 Kate Greenaway Medal

Through the changing seasons, James watches his farmer father at work and cannot wait for the day when he can be a farmer too.

"Illustrations that make you want to stroke the page, and a story of such family warmth and country charm you're left with a warm glow." *Books for Keeps*

0-7445-1762-1    £4.99

### MY FRIEND HARRY

James takes his toy elephant Harry everywhere – around the farm, on holiday, to bed… Then, one day, James starts school.

"An altogether charming picture book… Bound to be a much-returned-to-favourite with 3 – 6 year olds." *The Junior Bookshelf*

0-7445-5295-8    £4.99

### FIRST SNOW

Sara goes with Mummy, teddy and the dogs to feed the sheep one winter's morning and to her delight, it starts to snow.

"A delightful book for parents and younger children to share and for older children to linger over." *Children's Books of the Year*

0-7445-4325-8    £4.99